KAJIN
THE BEAST
CATCHER

BY ADAM BLADE

ORCHARD

TION

THE

THE RAINBOW JUNGLE

Dear Reader,

My hand shakes as I write. You find us in our hour of greatest peril.

My master Aduro has been snatched away. The kingdom is on its knees. Not one, but two enemies circle our shores – Kensa, the banished witch, has returned from Henkrall. With her stalks Sanpao, the Pirate King. Strange magic is afoot, stirring not just in Avantia but all the kingdoms, and I sense new Beasts lurking.

Only Tom and Elenna stand in the way of certain destruction. Can they withstand the awful test that will surely come? This time, courage alone may have to be enough.

Yours, in direst straits,

Daltec the apprentice

PROLOGUE

Freya paused on the edge of the
Rainbow Jungle. Everything appeared
peaceful in the rosy light of the
Gwildorian dawn. Still, Freya felt
ripples of tension in her muscles.
Only yesterday, she had been almost
killed by Solak, a strange shark Beast.
Long ago, Freya's husband, Taladon,
had imprisoned Solak and five other
terrible Beasts in the Lightning Prison.
Now Tom and Elenna had used the
Lightning Paths in their Quest against

the Evil Witch Kensa. This had caused the release of Solak – and maybe the other five Beasts as well. *Which means the kingdoms are in terrible peril*, Freya thought.

She listened to the chorus of birdsong that drifted from the tree canopy. The jungle shimmered with vivid yellow and emerald green. Scarlet flowers opened, releasing sweet perfume. Her horse, Flame, nibbled at the leaves of the small tree she had tied him to.

A groan interrupted Freya's thoughts. Someone was in trouble! She pushed through bushes laden with pink berries. A man sat slumped against a copper-coloured tree trunk. Freya rushed to him. His face was ghostly pale and beaded with sweat. He clutched at the shredded collar of

his tunic and Freya saw blood
seep between his fingers.

"You're wounded!" she said.
"Let me help you."

Kneeling, she unclenched the man's
fingers and pulled the tunic aside.
Deep wounds punctured his neck and
shoulders. "What happened to you?"
she gasped. But the man was too
weak to answer. Freya reached into

the pouch at her waist and removed a strip of linen. She moistened it in the dew that coated the leaves of the surrounding bushes, then she gently wiped the man's wounds and bandaged them.

What creature was responsible?

She made sure the man was comfortable, then stepped into the jungle. She was determined to find the creature that had done this.

Something glimmered on the moist ground. Broken shards of violet shell lay smeared with gooey yolk. Freya felt sick with regret and fear. Someone – or something – had mercilessly smashed one of the Good Beast Amictus's eggs.

"Who would have done this to something so beautiful?" Freya muttered.

The calm air was torn apart by a terrified scream.

The hair rose on Freya's neck and she plunged through the bushes. The scream grew louder, seeming to pierce Freya's skull. She burst out into bright sunshine.

Flame!

Freya's horse kicked and thrashed as he was pulled backwards inside a huge net. The tree he was tied to bent under the strain. The horse's leather reins were stretched taut.

"Let him go!" Freya ordered. At that instant, the reins snapped. Flame crashed onto his side with his hooves pawing the air. His struggling body was still being dragged across the grass. Freya began to run.

A shadow fell over her. She glanced up and staggered, flinging out an arm in protection. *The Beast has arrived,* she realized.

The creature was as tall as the trees, towering against the rising sun. His snout wrinkled back over sabre-like teeth as he growled. A shaggy grey pelt rippled over his chest. Long, jagged claws curled from his hands.

And held in its claws was the net that had caught Flame! It stretched between the Beast's hands and the screaming horse. Small objects, like gems, sparkled in the rope strands.

Why would there be gems in a net? Freya wondered. Squinting at the objects, she realized that they weren't gems at all. They were the claws and teeth of long-dead animals, sparkling because they were wet with dew – and with Flame's blood.

Freya drew her sword. She tried to

cut Flame free but the Beast yanked
on the net. With a triumphant roar,
he seized the horse and twirled

him over his head.

"Let him go!" Freya yelled.

The Beast's eyes lit up when he spotted her racing figure. She dodged in beneath the net and raised her sword. When she slashed open a corner of the net, Flame dropped through and landed with a thud.

"Run, Flame!" Freya called. The stallion staggered to his feet. His eyes rolled white with panic as the Beast roared and stretched out a hand. With a burst of speed, the stallion dodged clear and he galloped away in terror.

There was a moment's silence as the huge wolf-man glared at Freya. The ground vibrated as he strode towards her, licking his lips. His putrid breath cast a cloud that made her gag. She tried to grip the hilt of her sword but her arms shook and her blade wavered. The wolf-man's claws swiped downwards. In that instant, Freya knew she'd have to do something she'd never done before. She needed to send a message to her son, before her life ended.

Tom! Tom, I need your help!

CHAPTER ONE

AN URGENT MESSAGE

Tom jerked awake, images from his bad dream swirling in his head: Aduro's hands bound with a glowing chain…the severe faces of the other wizards…Aduro's lips croaking out the word 'guilty'.

I wish it really was only a dream, Tom thought as he kicked aside his blanket.

But it was true: Aduro had confessed to the Circle of Wizards that he had used the forbidden Lightning Path magic to send Tom and Elenna to Henkrall. There, they had defeated the Beasts of that kingdom. But the Evil Witch Kensa had followed them back to Avantia, using the Lightning Path. The damage caused by her arrival had released six new Beasts into Avantia and Gwildor. Now, Aduro was locked in a cell, punished for helping Tom on his Quest to defeat Kensa.

I have to fight the new Beasts before I can help Aduro, Tom thought grimly. *But I will help my old friend as soon as I possibly can!*

Tom rose stiffly to his feet, still tired from yesterday's battle against Solak, Scourge of the Sea. After rolling up his blanket, he straightened to look around. Elenna and his mother slept beside the ashes of a small fire. Inland, the dawn light streamed over hills of lush grass and flowers. Tom's stallion, Storm, grazed hungrily. He had been magically sent to Gwildor the previous evening along with Elenna's wolf, Silver. They had been greeted with a whinny by Freya's horse, Flame. This morning Tom couldn't see Flame anywhere. Perhaps the stallion was hidden by a grove of trees.

Tom turned towards the sea. Usually vast, it had shrunk to a narrow channel. Without even squinting, Tom could see the smudge of the Avantian shoreline. These kingdoms were usually separated by an ocean! Chaos had been unleashed, thanks to Tom and Elenna's use of the Lightning Path, and the kingdoms had been drawn together. Tom had never encountered so much terrible magic. Even though the scene looked peaceful in the golden rays of the sun, he knew he was surrounded on every side by evil.

But I will conquer this evil… I will make up for my mistakes, he thought.

Tom's stomach rumbled. They would all need to eat breakfast before beginning their Quest. Tom decided to collect driftwood and light a fire. He stepped around his mother's bed roll. At least he was reunited with her, so not everything was bad. If only his father was here too – then they'd be a family.

Tom pushed aside his grief over Taladon's death. Although he would always miss his father, he knew he must stay focused on the Quest. He stopped to pick up a piece of wood, then paused. Looking back at Freya's bed roll, he realised that there was no sign of a sleeping body beneath the blankets. Where was his mother?

"Elenna!" he cried. "Come quickly."

Elenna's dark head poked out from beneath her blanket, and Silver sprang up with a growl. Leaping to her feet, Elenna grabbed her bow. She notched an arrow and swung around, searching for the danger.

"Mother's bed is empty," Tom said.

Still holding an arrow ready, Elenna scanned the shoreline where ripples washed the sand and birds sailed on the breeze.

"I don't see any sign of enemies," she said at last.

"Neither do I. But where could my mother have gone?"

"She's probably out exercising her horse. They'll be back for breakfast. I'll roll up her bed." Elenna lowered her bow and pointed. "Tom, look."

Poking from beneath Freya's pillow was a scrap of parchment. Tom picked it up. His fingers throbbed as he gripped it and the scabs on his palms oozed clear fluid. He had been hurt on his last Quest and the wounds would probably leave scars. Tom couldn't even use his Phoenix talon to heal them. The talon, like the others tokens in his belt and shield, had been drained of power by the mysterious wizard known as the Judge. He had made that a condition of allowing Tom a chance to save Aduro from prison. Thank goodness he'd slipped the ruby jewel into his tunic – that was one magic power he still had.

Tom read the note scrawled on the scrap of parchment. *Couldn't sleep. Have gone to do a small patrol of the kingdom. Back soon. Freya.*

Tom frowned. How long ago had his mother left?

"Why—?" Pain hit him behind his eyes. He fell to his knees and clutched his temples.

The parchment fluttered to the ground.

"Tom, what's wrong?" Elenna asked, clutching his arm.

A dizziness that felt like magic surged through Tom's head.

Is someone trying to send me a message? Tom wondered. *Yes, it's coming from… my mother!*

A feeling of dread filled Tom's chest. He closed his eyes and waited for the dizziness to pass.

"My mother is in grave danger, I can feel it," Tom said. "She's desperate for help!"

"But we don't even know where she is!"

"Maybe Daltec's map can help us." Tom fumbled in his saddlebags and pulled out the scroll that the apprentice wizard had given him as a guide for his latest Quest. Tom was still trying to decide how good a guide Daltec was – the young wizard's spells didn't always work correctly. He would need years of practice before becoming as powerful and wise as Aduro.

Tom unrolled the scroll on the grass. A three dimensional map of the kingdom popped up to show tiny mountains, valleys and the thread of a twinkling river.

Elenna pointed at the map. "Look, a path is appearing!"

Tom watched as the path wound through the kingdom until it reached the Rainbow Jungle. His head cleared. "That's where my mother must be!"

Elenna looked puzzled. "But doesn't the path normally lead to the next Beast?"

"What else could be causing mother so much distress?" Tom said. "She must have encountered the Beast – and now she needs our help!"

Tom fumbled in his tunic pocket and pulled out a fragment of magic mirror, which Aduro had left in King Hugo's throne room. Although it only showed vague images, it could help Tom to track people. He watched

as images appeared: Freya's face
distorted by terror…rain dripping
from leaves…the flash of a parrot's
wing…a huge shadow with fangs and
curved claws.

"We must ride hard for the Rainbow
Jungle!" Tom yelled, stuffing the
mirror back into his pocket and
rolling up the map. He sprang onto
Storm, hauling Elenna up behind
him, and touched his heels to the
stallion's flanks.

Tom had already lost his father
on a Quest.

Mother, I won't lose you too!

CHAPTER TWO

FIRE ON THE HILLS

The sun rose higher in the sky as Storm cantered steadily to the south-west. Rolling farmland lay on either side of the track, and barley ripened in the fields.

Impatience gnawed at Tom. Despite Storm's efforts, it seemed as though they would never reach the Rainbow Jungle.

"We could travel so much faster with

the magic of Tagus's horseshoe token," Elenna said.

But the Judge – leader of the Circle of Wizards – had drained the power from that token too. Not for the first time, Tom wondered what the Judge's motives were. *Does he want me to succeed in my Quest to free Aduro? Or does the Judge have some secret grudge against him?*

When the sun was at its highest, they stopped at a village to rest Storm. Both animals drank from a stone trough in the village square. Tom's stomach growled with hunger and he wished they'd had time for a fire and some breakfast. They mounted again and rode until the sun sank and long shadows stretched across them. Darkness fell swiftly.

"Look ahead," Tom said suddenly.

He pointed to a twinkle of light on
a ridge of hills.

"Is that a camp fire?" Elenna asked.

"I think so." Tom patted Storm's neck
and encouraged him onwards. "Maybe
someone there will share food with us."

As they came closer, orange flames
leapt up, spitting showers of brilliant
sparks. The dark shapes of people
drifted around, throwing more logs
onto the fire. Beyond them stood a ring
of caravans. Their curved roofs and
brightly painted sides gleamed yellow,
red and green. Tom reined Storm to
a walk. "It's the wandering people,"
he said. "I don't think they'll do us
any harm."

"But why is their fire so huge?"
Elenna asked. "It's like the fire that
was used to imprison the Good Beast
Koldo."

Tom shuddered, remembering the Arctic Warrior's torment as he was bound with ropes and almost melted to death by fire. He reined Storm to a halt. *Maybe approaching this fire isn't a good idea.*

But the camp did seem peaceful. A smell of stew drifted in the air, and Tom's stomach growled again. He nudged Storm forward and Silver followed close at his heels.

Something hissed through the darkness.

"Look out!" Tom yelled, ducking.

Storm reared up, his neck banging into Tom's face. Pain exploded in Tom's nose, and tears flooded his eyes, blinding him as Storm plunged and fought. Elenna's arms tightened around his waist as Silver snarled in the direction the missile had come from.

Tom struggled to see beyond the fire, but he knew what that hissing noise had been – a lasso. The rope looped and pulled tight around Storm's neck. Shadowy figures hauled the stallion to a standstill. Other figures sprinted from between the caravans, and reached up to drag Tom and Elenna from the saddle. Tom sprawled on the grass. His hand grasped his sword but before he could unsheathe it, a man forced him down with a knee on his chest. A curved blade flashed. Tom felt the cold steel of a dagger pressed against his throat. In the leaping light, Tom glimpsed his attacker's long hair and patched yellow shirt.

Storm bucked on the end of his rope, dragging men across the grass. Elenna punched her captor as Silver bounded forward to defend her, but the man kicked out at him.

"Run, Silver!" Elenna screamed, and her wolf limped into the shadows.

Elenna's attacker clamped a brawny arm around her neck and squeezed.

"Let her go!" Tom yelled, squirming.

The man on Tom's chest pressed the dagger harder against his throat. "Save your breath," he snarled.

Tom saw that he had no choice, but his heart leapt as Elenna kicked her attacker in the shins. He hopped on the spot, howling, and with a final kick, Elenna tore free and snatched an arrow from her quiver.

"Drop your weapon or I slit your friend's throat," growled the man on Tom's chest.

Tom shook his head at Elenna. Her eyes blazed, but she understood Tom's warning. Slowly she lowered her bow.

The pressure of the blade eased on Tom's throat. "We do love a good tale," growled his captor. "So spin us a yarn about why you're skulking around our camp."

Tom's mind went blank. He didn't usually tell people about the Beasts. What tale could explain their presence in the Gwildorian hills?

"Can't think of a reason?" the man asked. He shook Tom until his head banged on the ground. "You're a little spying ferret is what you are!"

"We're not spying on you!" Elenna said. "We're travellers in need of a warm fire and some hot food."

"Maybe so, maybe not. But you children could have got yourselves killed wandering around. If not by us, then by…" – the wanderer's voice sank to a whisper – "…the wolf-man." The other men fell silent.

Wolf-man? Tom thought. *Our next Beast, more likely! But these people are nervous enough without me saying anything about the evil loose in Gwildor.*

Tom was released and he got to his feet. The man who'd been fighting with Elenna led Storm towards the caravans. He had calmed the stallion with soothing whispers.

"Hey! Bring back my horse!" Tom called.

"Keep your voice down!" the wanderer commanded, casting a glance into the darkness. "Follow me if you want something in your bellies."

Tom glanced at Elenna and she nodded. All he wanted to do was ride to the Rainbow Jungle and do battle with the Beast – after all, Aduro's life depended on Tom vanquishing the Beasts and capturing the Evil Witch Kensa and Sanpao the Pirate King. *But what choice do we have? These men have us at their mercy.* Reluctantly, he followed Elenna and the group to the fire.

Two children lay close to the flames, their bodies shaking and shivering.

Their skin shone with sweat. A woman knelt beside them, trying to spoon stew into their mouths. It dribbled out as they moaned and twitched.

No wonder the people are so jittery… Something is very wrong here, Tom thought.

The woman cast a miserable glance at Tom, her face shadowed by her embroidered shawl. She jerked her head in the direction of the pot nestled in the ashes.

"My children can't eat so you strangers may as well help yourselves," she said.

Elenna laid her hands on the children's foreheads. "They're burning with fever," she said. "If we could bring down their temperature, maybe they would eat."

"Easy for you to say!" the woman cried. "We daren't go collecting herbs to help with the fever. There's a giant wolf roaming about. Look what it did to my children!"

She pulled back the boy's tunic to reveal gaping wounds on his neck.

Tom's pulse raced. *They are teeth marks! Surely only a Beast could have inflicted such a wound.*

Elenna drew a roll of canvas from her pocket. Unfurling it, she removed strips of thin, dried bark. "This is from the white willow. If we brew it into a tea, it will lower your childrens' fevers. Then maybe they can eat and get better."

Tears of gratitude brimmed in the woman's eyes. She clasped Elenna's hands. "I'm sorry for being so angry. But I don't know if my children will live to see the dawn!"

CHAPTER THREE

GALLOPING INTO THE DARK

After reassuring the woman, Tom and Elenna went to get a bowl of stew each, and joined a man perched on a felled tree trunk.

"My name is Billy," the man said. "Some terrible creature attacked those children last night. It can't be a fox or a badger that made those bites. Only a wolf's teeth would leave such puncture holes."

"Is this why you've piled the fire so high?" Elenna asked.

"Yes. The wolves hate the flames. And we hate the wolves."

"You've obviously never spent time with a real wolf!" Elenna protested. "They're the most loyal creatures in the kingdom."

As Elenna spoke, Silver crept from the shadows. He pressed against Elenna's legs, whining in greeting.

Billy leapt to his feet with a roar, sending his stew bowl flying. "It's him – it's the wolf that attacked our children!"

Men surged forward. Some of them waved burning sticks snatched from the fire. Silver's hackles rose and he snarled, crouching against Elenna to protect her.

"Hush, Silver." Elenna smoothed Silver's forehead until his snarl sank to a whine.

Tom's eyes searched for the men who'd first attacked him and Elenna. They would know that Silver was a companion and not a wild creature. When Tom couldn't spot the men, he knew he'd have to prove Silver's innocence himself. He held out his hands. "Good people," he said, "Silver is our faithful friend. Look at his size. He's much too small to have made the wounds inflicted on those children."

"All wolves are cursed enemies! They sneak around our herds!" one man shouted. His black beard wagged angrily.

"And if this animal didn't attack our children, then what did?" another man asked, shaking a fist.

The ring of men crowded closer. Sparks showered from their burning sticks. Silver snarled again. Elenna knelt and circled her arms around his neck.

How can I calm them down and save Silver? Tom thought. He didn't normally talk about the Beasts, but knew that he had no choice.

"Please listen to me!" Tom said.

"It is not wolves, but Beasts that are abroad. An evil witch has brought terror to the kingdoms of Avantia and Gwildor. It is her Beasts that are wreaking havoc. She travels in a pirate's flying ship—"

Jeers and roars of laughter interrupted Tom. "Eh, lad?" yelled one man. "We'd have to be soft in the head to believe that nonsense."

"Save your fairytales for children!" yelled another.

The circle tightened around Silver and Elenna as black boots thumped forward.

"No man hurts my wolf!" Elenna cried. She reached for an arrow but Tom shook his head at her.

Suddenly a woman thrust through the crowd. She flung the shawl back from her head and Tom saw she was the mother of the wounded children. Her eyes flashed, and her silver arm rings jangled.

"The girl's herbs have helped my children!" she cried. "If any man harms her, or her companions, he'll feel the kiss of my blade!"

The woman yanked a glittering dagger from her belt and twirled it in one hand. The men backed away.

With a satisfied nod, she stooped to stroke Silver's head before returning to her children.

She must be the clan leader, Tom thought.

Billy ducked his head in apology. "Sorry about that, young strangers. Simple folk we are, more used to tales about cattle raids and horse fairs. But I can offer you a safe place to sleep tonight. My caravan is snug. Now that Ma Mollie has vouched for you both, we'll give you no more trouble."

"We need to continue our journey," Tom said.

"I won't hear of it. It's far too dangerous to be astray at night."

Tom's muscles burned with tiredness. Perhaps they should accept Billy's offer and rest for just a little while.

*No, the Beast stalks in the darkness.
We cannot rest until he's defeated and
my mother is saved!*

Tom waited until Billy stooped to
thrust a log into the fire. "Come on,"
Tom whispered to Elenna.

"Follow me," Elenna whispered to
Silver.

Silently they backed away from the fire.

"I've a fine feather bed…" Billy said,
still bent over the fire.

Tom and Elenna whirled and ran
towards the horses.

"Storm!" Tom called and his stallion
neighed in reply. A boy was grooming
his silky flanks. "Thank you for taking
care of Storm. But no more grooming
now!" Tom said and sprang onto his
horse's back.

Billy realised what was happening.
"You young fools, you come back

here! It's not safe outside," he called.

"Quick, Elenna!" Tom said, reaching down for her.

She jumped up behind Tom as Storm broke into a trot with Silver loping alongside.

"Take these!" Ma Mollie cried, running across the camp as Tom circled Storm towards the south-west. She thrust a bundle of candles into Elenna's hands. "Made them myself...put a few simple spells on them... They'll light your way in the darkness!" she panted.

"Thank you!" Elenna called as Tom urged Storm into a gallop. The stallion thundered into the hills.

Simple spells might not be enough, Tom thought. *I haven't any powers to battle this wolf-man with. Only my ability to communicate with Beasts...*

CHAPTER FOUR

A LIVING FORTRESS

A full moon rose over the hills as
Storm and Silver trotted along.
Dropping the reins, Tom pulled
Daltec's map from his tunic and
unfurled it. Tom peered at it by
the light of the moon.

"We're close to our destination," he
told Elenna. "Be ready for an attack
from the Beast."

Tom stowed the map away and

peered ahead. Gwildor's rolling countryside was washed by silver light. Up ahead, a mass of trees rose above the fields.

The Rainbow Jungle!

Tom's heart missed a beat. Somewhere in that inky wilderness lurked Kensa's next Beast, a creature with teeth that could pierce bone. The jungle stretched away in both directions and disappeared into the night. It was like a living fortress.

"I'd forgotten it was so huge," Elenna said. "I wonder which route we should take in."

As they got closer, Tom saw how tall the trees were. They towered against the stars, and blocked the moonlight from reaching the ground. Tom reined Storm to a halt and listened. A solitary bird screeched. Crickets chirped.

The air smelled of sweet flowers and rotting leaves.

Silver growled. "Look over there!" Elenna said, pointing towards some shrubs.

Two figures seemed to be struggling with each other.

Who are they? Tom wondered. *Has*

Kensa set a trap? Or do they need help?

Cautiously Tom nudged Storm forwards. Moonlight shone on the dark hair of a figure he instantly recognised. *That's my, my…*

"Mother!" Tom called.

The other figure had his arms around Freya.

She's being attacked! Tom thought.

"We need to help her!" Elenna cried.

Tom drew his sword and urged Storm on. The stallion raced across the grass, into the deep gloom cast by the jungle. Silver ran at his side, yelping.

As Storm skidded to a halt, Tom realized that his mother was not struggling against the other figure. She was helping the man to walk with an arm over his shoulder. His face was drained of all colour, and was taut with pain.

Tom sheathed his sword, and he and Elenna slid to the ground. Silver whined a greeting to Freya.

"I'm so glad you've come!" Freya said.

"Mother! What's happened?" Tom asked.

Freya's eyes were wide with fear. They didn't meet Tom's gaze but darted from tree to tree, shadow to shadow, as though she expected to be

attacked at any moment.

"It's the wolf-man…the terrible wolf-man!" the stranger babbled. He clutched at Freya for balance. The front of his tunic was stained with blood.

Elenna gently pulled the fabric aside to reveal puncture wounds just like those on the children.

"The pressure of my bandages caused him too much pain," Freya said. "He tore them off…" Her voice trailed away as she spun around, scanning the trees.

"Can you describe the creature for me?" Tom said.

The man's face contorted with panic. "A wolf's head, a man's body. He was carrying some sort of net, and his teeth were so huge that—"

His voice ended in a terrified gulp,

and his hands flew to his wounds.

He'll be fighting for his life, soon, Tom thought. *The poison will spread through his body.*

"Do you have a home and family to go to?" Elenna asked gently.

"I live in a hut away over the fields there. My wife will be worried about me." Sweat broke out on his forehead.

Tom reached into his saddlebag for a candle. He lit it with a flint and handed it to the man. "This will help you find your way home."

"And you will need to use white willow for your fever," Elenna said, hastily unrolling her canvas cloth. She pressed some strips of bark into the man's hand. "Your wife must boil this into a tea. Go home as fast as you can. You will need help to…recover."

The man seemed to notice Elenna

and Tom's sombre expressions, and
Freya's nervous eyes.

"Something's seriously wrong in
Gwildor, isn't it?" he asked.

"Yes," Tom said. "But we are going
to take care of it. If you head straight
home over the fields, away from the
jungle, you'll be safe."

"And where are you going?" the
man asked.

"Into the jungle," Tom said. His
hand gripped his sword.

The man gasped. "Good luck! You
are either brave or foolish!" Gripping
his willow bark, he staggered free of
Freya's arms.

"Thank you, good lady," he said
before hobbling away as fast as he
could.

Tom glanced around. "Where's
Flame?" He'd suddenly realised

that his mother's faithful horse was nowhere in sight.

"He fled in fear," Freya muttered. "My poor stallion, I failed him…" Her lips set into a thin line. "You can't face this Beast alone, Tom."

"But it's my Quest!" he said. He didn't want to put anyone in any more danger.

"Maybe we should wait until morning," Elenna suggested. "It's pitch black in the jungle. How will we see where—"

There was a swishing noise through the trees.

"Watch out!" Tom shouted. They all jumped backwards. Something whooshed through the air and landed at Tom's feet with a thud. He bent to examine it. He recognised the tiny creature from his fight against

another Beast. The insect's four fragile,
shimmering wings were crushed,
and its barbed tail was snapped off. It
scrabbled at the ground with spindly
legs as it died.

"It's one of the Good Beast Amictus's
baby bugs!" he exclaimed.

"Poor little thing! Who would fling it through the air like that?" Elenna asked.

"This is the work of the Beast," Freya said. "He must be close by and we'll soon be able to fight him."

Tom pulled out his scroll and unfurled it. Inscribed across the magical map was a new name.

"Kajin," Tom said. "That's it. We can't wait for dawn. We need to go into the jungle now. There's a Beast waiting for us!"

CHAPTER FIVE

A STRANDED SHIP

"We'll come back for you soon," Tom said, slapping Storm's hide to send him into a clearing.

"Stay together," Elenna commanded Silver. The wolf lay down at Storm's hooves as Tom, Elenna and Freya turned to face the Rainbow Jungle. Tom ducked in past the first trees. He tripped over a gnarled root and flung out a hand for balance. Thorns slashed his fingertips and he jerked his hand back. Warm air pressed around him. He knew how hostile this jungle could be, but they had to press on. *While there's blood in my veins, I will come face-to-face with Kajin.* Just the sound of the Beast's name, rolling around inside his head, made him shudder.

The moonlight faded as they pressed deeper into the jungle. Tom glanced up and saw a web of giant creepers snaking between the trees. As thick as Tom's arm, they coiled around everything in their path and created a canopy above them.

Tom swatted at the whining mosquitoes that hovered in a dense cloud. They darted in to sting his cheeks.

"Let's use Mollie's candles," Elenna suggested. She pulled a flint from her quiver and struck a spark to light the candle wicks. The flames puffed out blue smoke that smelled like lavender, and the mosquitoes faded back into the trees.

"Mollie must have put a smoke spell on these candles," Elenna said. "They've got rid of the bugs, but they don't really light our way."

"For all I can tell, we're walking in circles," Tom agreed.

"I'll start making marks." Freya used her sword tip to notch a cut into a

tree. "If we see this again, we'll know we're circling around."

Their progress through the jungle was slow. They pushed and pulled each other over rotting logs, and stooped beneath hanging creepers. Their boots slipped on rotting leaves. High overhead, a breeze stirred the thick canopy with a mournful sigh.

Tom's hand tightened on his sword as he stumbled to the edge of a large clearing. A huge shape loomed in the centre, tilted over at an angle. Tom glimpsed a jutting bowsprit, a rusty dangling anchor, and King Hugo's crest painted on the cabin door. "It's the Avantian ship!" he said in awe. He remembered how he and Elenna had first found the ship on a day of sunshine and brilliant colours when they'd come here to do battle with

Amictus the Bug Queen. They'd
liberated her and had been happy to
leave the Rainbow Jungle, knowing
that she would protect this part of
Gwildor. What a long time ago that
seemed now.

"Perhaps my rosewood arrow will still be there!" Elenna jumped past Tom, grinning. They'd left behind her arrowhead in exchange for some gold coins and a magical telescope they'd found. Elenna started to stride through the foliage when something moved on the ship.

"Don't!" Tom grabbed Elenna's arm and dragged her behind a tree. He blew out their candles. In the pitch darkness, he strained to hear any sounds from the ship.

"Pieces of eight!" said a voice through the darkness, followed by the screech of a parrot.

Tom edged his head around the tree trunk until he could see the ship again. Men swarmed along its mossy deck, climbed its cannons, and jumped through yawning hatchways. Tom saw the flash of a cutlass, and the flap of a pigtail. Moonlight reflected on a red neckerchief.

"Sanpao's pirates!" Tom whispered. "What are they doing here?"

"If they're here, Sanpao will be close by," Freya said.

Elenna pressed against Tom's shoulder to peek around the tree. "The pirates must be stealing the ship's supplies," she said. "I bet they won't leave anything in return."

"We never did discover how the Avantian ship came to be here," Tom said. If the kingdoms of Avantia and Gwildor had moved close together during this Quest, maybe...

"Perhaps the two kingdoms have drawn close together before now," Elenna suggested, saying exactly what Tom was thinking.

"You might be right," Tom said. But there wasn't time to think about this more. *If pirates are looting the ship, Sanpao must be close by – and maybe Kensa too. What evil are they up to?*

From his pocket, Tom pulled the grey gemstone that Daltec had given him. Its dull surface began to glow with red light, warning that Kensa was very near. The Circle of Wizards had charged him with capturing her, in exchange for Aduro's freedom.

But another Beast was getting in the way. Tom felt torn in two by this Quest. He couldn't ignore a Beast, but every battle got in the way of his pursuit of Kensa – and her capture was all that would guarantee Aduro's freedom. *What's more important, defeating Beasts or rescuing my old friend?* Even as Tom thought this, he knew what was most important – to save the kingdoms from the Beasts. *I'm sorry, Aduro. I have to do this.*

"Let's leave the pirates to their looting," Tom said, turning to the others. "At least it's keeping them busy. We have more important things to worry about."

Tom thrust the gemstone back into his pocket and led the way deeper into the jungle. He kept one hand outstretched to pull back low branches and twining creepers. Something began to glow up ahead. A violet shimmer lit the base of tree trunks.

Tom crept closer, testing every step before putting his weight down. He held his breath. A trail of shining purple eggs wound across the fallen leaves and damp ground like a path of pearls.

"Amictus's eggs," Tom whispered when Elenna and Freya crept beside him.

"Not just the eggs," Freya hissed. She pointed at two figures, their silhouettes silver-lined in the moonlight.

Leaning over the eggs were two
faces, their grins lit by the purple
glow. The woman's swirling robe
was decorated with symbols of cogs,
wheels, arrows and stars. Its hem
brushed against the eggs.

Kensa and Sanpao! Tom thought.
*We've found them at last. Now where is
the Beast?*

CHAPTER SIX

NEEDLESS DEATH

Tom stepped closer, keeping in the shadows of dangling vines.

"…worth a hundred weight in gold!" Kensa cackled, rubbing her bony hands together.

"But I spotted them first!" roared Sanpao, squinting at the glowing eggs.

"If it wasn't for me, you'd still be mouldering in King Hugo's dungeons. So if anyone should take these eggs,

77

it's me!" The witch's voice rose to a
shriek and sparks crackled in her hair.

Sanpao stretched out a hand over
the lavender eggs.

*How dare they threaten the babies of a
Good Beast?* Tom thought. He flung the
vines aside. "Don't touch those eggs!"
he yelled.

Without a moment's hesitation,
Sanpao reached into the top of
his high black boot. He snatched
something out and hurled it straight at
Tom's heart. Its deadly point flashed.

Tom flung himself sideways into a patch of bushes, raising a cloud of moths. Sanpao's dagger embedded itself into a tree trunk.

Tom thrashed free of the bushes and stood up.

Kensa's lips curled in a sneer. "So, the little boy is playing with toys too big for him," she mocked.

A hot wave of anger rose in Tom's chest. He fought it down and tried to think clearly. He had no magic jewels other than the ruby, and no power in his shield tokens. If he was to battle Kensa and Sanpao, he would have to do it hand-to-hand. *At least Elenna and Freya will help*. But when Tom glanced around, he didn't see them. Maybe they were staying hidden and preparing for a surprise attack.

Tom reached for his sword and

gasped in pain as he pulled it out. The scabs on his wounded hands had broken open again.

Kensa raised her heavy metal staff into the air. Tom knew the power the staff wielded – he had seen her use it to travel the Lightning Path.

Sanpao drew another dagger from his belt. Its serrated, curving edge gleamed blue.

"This blade loves to kiss the necks of fools," Sanpao said.

For a long moment, no one moved. Tom wondered if his mother and Elenna might jump out from behind their tree. But they didn't join him. He edged his blade higher, ready to block an attack. *Do your worst*, he thought. *I'm ready!* He lunged forwards with his blade and was surprised to see Kensa and Sanpao share a glance and a nod, and then suddenly duck back into the jungle, rather than meet his attack. *What's happening? Why aren't they fighting?*

Sanpao gave a long, shrill whistle through his teeth and looked up between the trees.

Tom tensed, his heart pounding. Suddenly, the moonlight was blotted out as something passed over it. The pirate ship! It was sailing overhead. Treetops scraped its hull. A rope snaked down between the tangle of creepers to dangle in mid-air.

"So long, landlubber!" the pirate king yelled at Tom.

"Cowards!" Tom called, running forwards. Too late. In one swift move, Sanpao snatched up one of Amictus's eggs and darted to the rope. He shimmied up it with the egg beneath one arm.

Tom tried to block Kensa's escape, but he was forced to jump clear when she swiped her mighty staff. By the time Tom had found his footing again, the witch was climbing the rope.

"Remember, half that egg is mine!" she said, jabbing at Sanpao with the point of her staff.

The pirate ignored her. He slashed at creepers with his dagger, hacking a space large enough for himself and Kensa to climb through. Tom tried to snatch the end of the rope but Kensa yanked it up, coiling it over her staff.

"That egg—" Kensa shrieked.

"Will not be even one-quarter yours if you jab me again!" roared the pirate. He swiped hard at a thick creeper. The egg slipped from his arm and plummeted towards the ground, bouncing off branches.

"You clumsy rat!" the witch yelled.
Do they ever stop arguing? Tom
thought. He sheathed his sword and

leapt forwards, arms outstretched.

But he was too late. The lavender egg smashed into the ground with a heavy thump and split open. Splinters of shell flew into the air and gooey yolk spilled onto the ferns.

"No!" Tom called. He knew how precious these eggs were.

It was all over. Kensa and Sanpao had slipped from his grasp and another of Amictus's babies had been sacrificed.

There was only one thing left to do – only one thing that Tom could do.

He turned to face the densest part of the jungle. "I'm coming to get you, Kajin," he called.

CHAPTER SEVEN

A SHADOW ACROSS THE MOON

There was just one mystery Tom needed to solve first. His eyes scanned the massive trees.

"Elenna? Mother?" he called. It was strange that they were still keeping out of sight. Normally, they would have rushed to Tom's side to help him in any battle, no matter how frightening.

"Mother?" Tom called again, more

loudly. "Elenna!"

Warm, silent air pressed around Tom but his heart felt cold with fear. He rushed back to where he'd left his mother and best friend crouching. The spot was empty. Tom looked around, searching the ground. Long tracks had been scraped into the moss and ferns lay broken. Some kind of fight had taken place!

"Tom!"

The cry drifted from high overhead. Tom flung back his head and peered into the thick gloom. Two figures struggled above his head. Freya and Elenna were suspended in a net woven with claws and teeth from long-dead animals. Tom recoiled in disgust.

The more Elenna and Freya thrashed, the more entangled they became in the net. Tom saw strands of rope coiled around Elenna's arms and his mother's legs.

"Stay still!" he called. "I'll climb up and cut you free."

Tom grasped the shaggy bark of a tree and began to haul himself up, pushing aside sharp-edged leaves.

A drawn-out howl shattered the night air. Tom froze, the hairs on his

neck standing up as he clung to a branch. Above Tom lurched a giant man with a wolf's head! Tom saw pricked ears and a long snout. A grey shaggy pelt covered the wolf-man's broad chest, and shone in the moonlight. One hand, tipped with yellow curling claws, held the net.

Kajin!

The Beast's eyes glowed and swivelled toward Tom. With a snarl, Kajin swiped downwards and hit Tom. The blow's force broke Tom's grip on the branch and he let go. He hurtled through the air and leaves sliced his cheeks. The jungle floor rushed up to smash his bones. *This is it!* Tom thought.

But before Tom crashed into the dirt, Kajin caught him in his giant hand. The Beast opened his fist. Tom scrambled to his feet on the yellow

palm and found himself face-to-face
with the wolf-man, close enough to
feel a blast of foul breath. There was
a stench of rotten meat and dark,
decaying things. Kajin's lips drew back,
revealing ferocious fangs that gleamed
like stone in the moonlight. Each

91

tooth was as long as Tom.

Kajin's eyes were golden slits, blazing with cunning and cruelty.

Tom slipped his hand into a pocket and held the ruby jewel. *I need to know what this Beast is thinking – this magic is the only advantage I have.* For a moment he heard nothing, only the squeaking of bats. Then Kajin's thoughts became clear.

The son of Taladon must die!

Tom gulped and let go of the jewel. The Beast was as evil as he'd feared!

Kajin's claws closed over Tom's head. He swung Tom into the air and drew his hand back over his shoulder. Tom realized that Kajin was going to fling him through the jungle.

Instinctively, Tom grasped at the tip of the wolf's ear and wrapped his fingers around the shaggy grey hair. As Kajin hurled his fist forward, Tom was yanked free and was left dangling from its ear. The Beast's howl of pain sent birds wheeling in fright.

Tom hauled himself through the wolf's pelt, hand over hand, and dropped into the dark cavern of Kajin's ear. His boots slipped on a thick coating of brown wax, and he had to grab another handful of hair to hold himself upright. He cautiously pulled himself higher. Even the hair he grabbed hold of was coated in wax, and Tom's wounded hands burned with pain.

Peering out, Tom saw Elenna and Freya dangling below in the net, half upside down. Far below were the clearing and the rotting hull of the Avantian ship.

How am I going to get all three of us back down? And how am I going to defeat this Beast?

CHAPTER EIGHT

TRAPPED BETWEEN TWO BEASTS

Amictus! Tom thought. *I can call on her for help with my red jewel!*

As guardian of Gwildor's Rainbow Jungle, the giant insect would want to come to Tom's aid, especially after Kajin had destroyed her eggs. He slipped one hand into his pocket and grasped the gemstone tightly. But then he realised, if he called on

Amictus, Kajin would also hear his
message. The wolf-man would be
warned that help was coming. Tom's
shoulders drooped. He couldn't risk
endangering the Bug Queen.

I have to fight this battle alone. He let
go of the jewel. Maybe this was the
time to use a Lightning Token. Still
clinging on to Kajin's greasy hair, Tom
shoved a fist into the bag at his side
and slipped out a token, hurling it
into the depths of the Beast's smelly

ear. As the gem exploded, a shock wave of sound blasted past Tom. Kajin lurched with a howl of pain.

Struggling on the waxy slope, Tom hauled himself higher until he was standing on the rim of Kajin's ear. He scanned the surrounding jungle for an escape route. Kajin continued to moan, bending over in pain.

"Look down," Freya called from where she and Elenna still swung in the net. "There's a nest below you."

An ancient, twisted tree with slippery grey bark was beside Kajin's shoulder. A fork in the branches held the spiky platform of an abandoned bird's nest. Perhaps Freya was right and Tom could use that…

He scrambled onto Kajin's sloping shoulder and climbed down hand over hand. He took a deep breath,

summoning his courage. Kajin
lurched closer to the nest, swatting
his injured ear.

Now!

Tom launched himself into the air,
his hands outstretched to grasp at
the ancient tree. Its branches swayed
beneath his weight as he landed.
Quickly he shimmied down until his
feet thumped into the nest, sinking
into feathers and empty nut shells.

Tom glanced around, breathing
hard. He ducked down as Kajin swung
round, his claws raking the air. The
last thing Tom needed was for the
Beast to notice him making an escape.

"Let us go, you brute!" Elenna
screamed at Kajin, distracting him.
She thrashed in the net so that it
rocked in Kajin's hand, bashing
against foliage and sending a shower

of nuts thumping to the jungle floor.
Kajin bent over the net, snarling.

Clever, Elenna! Tom thought. *While
Kajin is busy, I'll summon Amictus.
Hopefully Kajin wouldn't hear the
message being sent out above the sound
of his own roars.*

Again, Tom grasped the jewel of
Torgor and concentrated on sending
his thoughts into the darkness. *The
Rainbow Jungle is threatened. Amictus,
we need your help!*

Tom could only hope that the Bug
Queen had heard. Now he needed
to work out how to free Elenna and
Freya. He lowered himself over the
side of the nest and climbed down.
As he neared the ground, Amictus's
eggs lit his way with their violet glow.
Almost there! Tom's boot rested on a
piece of orange fungus – but it gave

way. For a moment, Tom swung by one hand, then his hold slipped and he fell into the shimmering glow.

With a sickening crack, Tom landed on an egg. He rolled away and jumped to his feet. In horror, he stared as the split-open egg. A green baby insect struggled out, pulling itself free with spiny legs. Was it injured? Tom held his breath. One of the baby's fragile wings was twisted. Tom felt a surge of guilt. He held out a hand, trying to lift the baby and help it become airborne.

Tree limbs cracked behind him. Tom spun around with the baby bug on his palm. Amictus! She had come to help them! Her great legs, with their lethal barbed spikes, scuttled through the scattered leaves. When she saw her injured baby, her angry shriek shattered

the stillness. She lunged forward.

The wolf-man pricked up his ears
and turned around. His eyes glowed.

Tom was trapped between two
Beasts!

CHAPTER NINE

MIGHTY FOES

Bravely, the baby insect took off and flapped awkwardly towards Amictus. It struggled to straighten its twisted wing, and then all four wings began to beat in time. With a trill of joy, the baby circled its mother's giant head.

Thank goodness – the injury was temporary! Tom felt a moment's relief.

A cloud slid over the moon,

plunging the jungle into darkness. Only the glimmering eggs lit Amictus's barbed legs and her armour of shiny skin.

"Tom, help!" Elenna cried.

A blast of foul air whooshed against Tom. He gagged and flung himself backwards. Just in time! Kajin's curved claws raked the air where Tom had been moments before. The ground shook as Amictus raised her own claws and aimed clubbing blows at Kajin.

Snarling, the wolf-man ducked. He swiped at the Bug Queen's muscular legs, making her stagger backwards and crash into a tree. Kajin swiped a fist towards Amictus's chest. Just in time, the insect lifted her limbs to block.

Tom's mind raced. *Kajin seems to*

have grown stronger since the moon was covered by a cloud. Perhaps he attacks at night because he doesn't like the light!

The clouds drifted on and faint moonbeams dappled the struggling Beasts. Tom glanced up at the thick

canopy of creepers. He remembered
the space that Sanpao had hacked
away during his escape. *If I clear more
leaves away then more moonlight will
reach us and Kajin will become weaker.*

Tom knew he'd need help to hack
a hole in the dense vines. Peering
into the gloom, he saw that Kajin
had hung his net over a high branch.
Inside the net, Elenna and Freya still
struggled, their faces and hands were
bleeding. The claws and bones were
slicing their skin. Tom wondered how
he could free them without injuring
himself.

He snatched at a trailing vine and
hauled himself up into a tree which
grew spiny fruit. Holding onto a
branch, Tom unsheathed his sword.

"Keep back from me," he whispered
to the others. "I don't want to

injure you." Elenna and his mother scrambled back in the net. He leant far out, hoping to shove the tip of the blade towards the net. *Closer. Closer...* With a thrill of triumph, he snagged the sword tip into the net. Leaning back and straining every muscle, Tom used his sword to swing the net towards him.

The blade sawed at the tough strands and clanked against the bones that were woven into the squares of netting. Suddenly, the fibres of the net gave way and a hole gaped open.

"Get ready," Tom warned, glancing down, hoping to see something that might break their fall. Only a row of eggs glowed below. Tom groaned. "Not again!" he muttered. Now was no time to distract Amictus from her fight with Kajin!

As he looked over, he saw Amictus raise a barbed limb and swipe it at Kajin, knocking him in the side of the head where the lightning token had exploded in his ear. The Evil Beast roared with pain and he bent over, crashing his skull into a tree. He leant back and his hairy chest was exposed. Amictus kicked the other Beast.

You're winning, Amictus! Tom thought. *Keep going!*

Tom struggled to haul the net closer to his own tree so that Elenna and Freya could climb out. He heard a tearing sound as more strands of the net began to break. Tom heaved, straining to swing the net closer, but he was too slow. The net broke apart, and a hole yawned open.

"No!" Tom cried.

Freya and Elenna plunged down

and shattered the eggs. Baby insects
rose into the air around them with
a loud buzz.

They swarmed towards Kajin.

"It's alright. The babies are not
injured!" Elenna shouted in relief.

"They must have been ready to
hatch!" Tom gasped. He watched as
the babies dived at Kajin, jabbing
the Beast with their leg spikes. Kajin
howled in pain and frustration and
staggered clumsily through the

undergrowth, swatting at bugs while Amictus advanced with her claws raised.

"Now we need to cut away the creepers and let the moonlight shine in!" Tom called.

"I can use my sword," Freya replied. She began climbing a nut tree to one side of Tom.

Elenna picked another tree and pulled herself into it. "Here's the dagger that Sanpao threw!" she said. She yanked the blade free and shoved it into her quiver before climbing on.

Tom began to climb too. Soon all three of them had reached the tangled creepers and begun to slash at them. Far below, Tom could hear the deadly fight continuing. Amictus groaned in pain and Tom knew there was no time to lose. *Kajin must not win!* Tom swung his sword back and forth, cleaving vines apart.

Finally they had cleared a ragged hole in the creepers. Soft silver light poured through it. If only the last clouds would sail clear of the moon...

"Now we have a chance of winning!" Tom cried. "You two stay here – I'm going to help Amictus!"

He dropped though the branches. As his feet thudded onto the ground, a roar vibrated the air. Tom turned and locked eyes with Kajin, who was lurching towards him.

Good, Tom thought. *Now it's my turn to fight the Beast!*

CHAPTER TEN

SPEARED THROUGH THE HEART

Kajin's lips wrinkled in a snarl as he strode across the trampled ferns. His huge hands swiped through the humid air.

Tom stepped into the middle of the clearing. He stood directly in the pool of moonbeams that shone through the hole he'd made in the creepers. His heart thundered.

Amictus paused near the ship's hull, as though realising that this fight belonged to Tom.

Kajin loomed over him, his snout raised as he gave an eerie howl. His fangs gleamed as he reached for the broken net and snatched it from the trees. His eyes glittered with cunning as he whirled the ropes over his head, the claws and bones shining in the moonlight. As the net fell in a glittering arc, Tom darted between Kajin's legs. He grabbed handfuls of grey hair and climbed the back of the Beast's legs.

"Not such a great shot with the net, are you?" Tom jeered. The Beast may not have been able to understand his words, but Tom could tell that his mocking tone was making Kajin angry. He staggered in circles, swatting at his own back as Tom scrambled higher up his leg, dodging claws.

Panting with effort, Tom pulled himself onto Kajin's head. At that moment, the last cloud drifted from the face of the moon. A burst of dazzling moonlight poured over the Beast. Tom grabbed fistfuls of pelt and tugged with all his might. The Beast roared in anger but did not lift his snout.

"Use your sword!" Freya called up, as she and Elenna watched. "Do what you have to."

Tom drew his sword and smashed the flat of the blade against the Beast's head.

Kajin threw his head back in pain. His eyes glittered in the moonlight and he squeezed them shut. Light gleamed on his broad forehead, and on the tips of his ears. His wet nose glistened.

With an echoing cry, the Beast fell to his knees. Elenna and Freya only just had time to leap out from their tree and scramble out of the way.

Trees shuddered. Nuts and berries

rained down. Bats swirled up, squeaking in terror.

Tom clung on as the Beast swayed to and fro. Blood trickled from the wounds on Tom's hands. It made Kajin's fur slippery. *I can't hold on much longer.*

Losing his balance, Kajin pitched forward. His mighty body fell towards the dark bulk of the Avantian ship. One of the masts – as long and thin as a spear – angled up from the sagging hull. The Beast toppled onto it. Tom felt the judder as it pierced the Beast's thick hide and he jumped to the ground. The mast's length plunged through Kajin's chest and impaled the Beast's heart. An anguished howl exploded from his mouth. The ship rocked.

Crouching nearby, Tom held his breath. *Is it over?*

The Beast seemed to shrink and
fade, his grey fur drifting away. His
teeth dropped to the ground with dull
thuds. They gleamed on the moss,
then vanished as though they had
never existed. Briefly, the Beast's
golden eyes hung in mid-air. Then

they blinked out. The ghostly shape of his body wafted away like mist.

"He's defeated!" Elenna whooped. She raced across the clearing with Freya behind her, and they flung their arms around Tom. As he felt himself caught up in a fierce hug, Tom looked at the broken ship and the space where Kajin's body had been, only a moment before. It was amazing that such a fierce Beast could be defeated so quickly. *If you just know the right way*, Tom thought, *and are brave enough*. The kingdoms were rid of one more evil Beast, which meant that Kensa's power was getting weaker. Tom was one step closer to fulfilling his promise to the Judge and bargaining for Aduro's freedom. *You're in my heart, old friend*. Tom hoped the Good Wizard would hear his silent message.

Baby insects danced overhead, trilling in glee. Tom pulled away from the embrace of Elenna and looked for the babies' mother. *There!* Even in the moonlight, Amictus's green skin made her almost invisible against the jungle foliage – but Tom could make out the look in her eyes, that brimmed with pleasure.

He clutched the gem in his pocket and sent one last message. *Thank you for coming to our aid, Good Beast of Gwildor.*

The giant insect dipped her head in understanding. Then she swiped branches aside and turned to stride into the jungle's depths. Her babies circled after her, their buzz growing faint.

"Time for us to leave, too," Elenna said.

"Our animals are waiting for us," Tom agreed. When he saw the sadness in Freya's face, he knew she was missing her faithful stallion. He laid an arm around his mother's shoulders.

"No more animals will be terrified, and no more will lose their lives!" he vowed. "While there is blood in my veins, I will fight the evil set loose by Sanpao and Kensa."

Freya smiled. "Your father would be proud," she said softly.

"Listen!" Elenna said.

Tom cocked his head. Faintly he heard Storm's neigh of welcome, and Silver's excited howl.

"Come on!" Tom broke into a run with Freya and Elenna close behind him. "Our next Quest will need all of us to work together!"

Join Tom on the next stage
of the Beast Quest when he meets

ISSRILLA
THE CREEPING
MENACE

Win an exclusive
Beast Quest T-shirt and goody bag!

In every Beast Quest book the Beast Quest logo is
hidden in one of the pictures. Find the logos in books
67 to 72 and make a note of which pages they appear
on. Write the six page numbers on a postcard and
send it in to us.
Each month we will draw one winner to receive
a Beast Quest T-shirt and goody bag.

THE BEAST QUEST COMPETITION:
THE DARKEST HOUR
Orchard Books
338 Euston Road, London NW1 3BH
Australian readers should email:
childrens.books@hachette.com.au

New Zealand readers should write to:
Beast Quest Competition
4 Whetu Place, Mairangi Bay, Auckland, NZ
or email: childrensbooks@hachette.co.nz

Only one entry per child.
Final draw: January 2014

You can also enter this competition
via the Beast Quest website: www.beastquest.co.uk

Join the Quest,
Join the Tribe

www.beastquest.co.uk

Have you checked out the Beast Quest website?
It's the place to go for games, downloads, activities,
sneak previews and lots of fun!

You can read all about your favourite Beasts,
download free screensavers and desktop wallpapers
for your computer, and even challenge your friends
to a Beast Tournament.

Sign up to the newsletter at www.beastquest.co.uk
to receive exclusive extra content and the
opportunity to enter special members-only
competitions. We'll send you up-to-date info on all
the Beast Quest books, including the next exciting
series which features six brand-new Beasts!

Get 30% off all Beast Quest Books at www.beastquest.co.uk
Enter the code BEAST at the checkout.

Offer valid in UK and ROI, offer expires December 2013

All books priced at £4.99.
Special bumper editions priced at £5.99.

Orchard Books are available from all good bookshops, or can
be ordered from our website: www.orchardbooks.co.uk,
or telephone 01235 827702, or fax 01235 8227703.

FREE COLLECTOR CARDS INSIDE!

Series 12: THE DARKEST HOUR
COLLECT THEM ALL!

Three lands are in terrible danger from six new
Beasts. Tom must ride to the rescue!

SOLAK
SCOURGE OF THE SEA

978 1 40832 396 0

KAJIN
THE BEAST CATCHER

978 1 40832 397 7

ISSRILLA
THE CREEPING MENACE

978 1 40832 398 4

VIGRASH
THE CLAWED EAGLE

978 1 40832 399 1

MIRKA
THE ICE HORSE

978 1 40832 400 4

KAMA
THE FACELESS BEAST

978 1 40832 401 1

OUT NOVEMBER 2012!

MEET A NEW HERO OF AVANTIA

ISBN: 978 1 4083 1 868 3

Dark magic has been unleashed!

Evil boy-Wizard Maximus is using the stolen golden gauntlet to wreak havoc on Avantia. A new hero must stand up to him, and battle the Beasts!

Read on for an exclusive extract of
CEPHALOX THE CYBERSQUID!

THE MERRYN TOUCH

The water was up to Max's knees and still rising. Soon it would reach his waist. Then his chest. Then his face.

I'm going to die down here, he thought.

He hammered on the dome with all his strength, but the plexiglass held firm.

Then he saw something pale looming through the dark water outside the submersible. A long, silvery spike. It must be the squid-creature, with one of its weird robotic attachments. Any second now it would smash the glass and finish him off...

There was a crash. The sub rocked. The silver spike thrust through the broken plexiglass. More water surged in. Then the spike withdrew and the water poured in faster. Max forced his way against the torrent to the opening. If he could just squeeze through the gap...

The jet of water pushed him back. He took one last deep breath, and then the water was over his head.

He clamped his mouth shut, struggling forwards, feeling the pressure on his lungs build.

Something gripped his arms, but it wasn't the squid's tentacle – it was a pair of hands, pulling him through the hole. The broken plexiglass scraped his sides and then he was through.

The monster was nowhere to be seen. In the dim underwater light, he made out the face of his rescuer. It was the Merryn girl, and next to her was a large silver swordfish.

She smiled at him.

Max couldn't smile back. He'd been saved from a metal coffin, only to swap it for a watery one. The pressure of the ocean squeezed him on every side. His lungs felt as though they were bursting.

He thrashed his limbs, rising upwards. He looked to where he thought the surface was, but saw nothing, only endless water. His cheeks puffed with the effort to hold in air. He let some of it out slowly, but it only made him want to breathe in more.

He knew he had no chance. He was too deep, he'd never make it to the surface in time. Soon he'd no longer be able to hold his breath. The water would swirl into his lungs and he'd die here, at the bottom of the sea. *Just like my mother*, he thought.

The Merryn girl rose up beside him, reached out and put her hands on his neck. Warmth seemed to flow from her fingers. Then the warmth turned to pain. What was happening? It got worse and worse, until Max felt as if his throat was being ripped open. Was she trying to kill him?

———

He struggled in panic, trying to push her off. His mouth opened and water rushed in.

That was it. He was going to die.

Then he realised something – the water was cool and sweet. He sucked it down into his lungs. Nothing had ever tasted so good.

He was breathing underwater!

He put his hands to his neck and found two soft, gill-like openings where the Merryn girl had touched him. His eyes widened in astonishment.

The girl smiled.

Other strange things were happening. Max found he could see more clearly. The water seemed lighter and thinner. He made out the shapes of underwater plants, rock formations and shoals of fish in the distance, which had been invisible before. And he didn't feel as if the ocean was crushing him any more.

Is this what it's like to be a Merryn? he wondered.

"I'm Lia," said the girl. "And this is Spike." She patted the swordfish on the back and it nuzzled against her.

"Hi, I'm Max." He clapped his hand to his mouth in shock. He was speaking the same strange language of sighs and whistles he'd heard the girl use when he first met her – but now it made sense, as if he was born to speak it.

"What have you done to me?" he said.

"Saved your life," said Lia. "You're welcome, by the way."

"Oh – don't think I'm not grateful – I am. But – you've turned me into a Merryn?"

The girl laughed. "Not exactly, but I've given you some Merryn powers. You can breathe underwater, speak our language, and your senses are much stronger. Come on – we need to get away from here. The Cyber Squid may come back."

In one graceful movement she slipped onto Spike's back. Max clambered on behind her.

"Hold tight," Lia said. "Spike – let's go!"

Max put his arms around the Merryn's waist. He was jerked backwards as the swordfish shot off through the water, but he managed to hold on.

They raced above underwater forests of gently waving fronds, and hills and valleys of rock. Max saw giant crabs scuttling over the seabed. Undersea creatures loomed up – jellyfish, an octopus, a school of dolphins – but Spike nimbly swerved round them.

"Where are we going?" Max asked.

"You'll see," Lia said over her shoulder.

"I need to find my dad," Max said. The crazy things that had happened in the last few moments had driven his father from his mind. Now it all came flooding back. Was his dad gone for good? "We have to do something! That monster's got my dad – and my dogbot too!"

"It's not the Cyber Squid who wants your father. It's the Professor who's *controlling* the Cyber Squid. I tried to warn you back at the city – but you wouldn't listen."

"I didn't understand you then!"

"You Breathers don't try to understand – that's your whole problem!"

"I'm trying now. What is that monster? And who is the Professor?"

"I'll explain everything when we arrive."

"Arrive where?"

The seabed suddenly fell away. A steep valley sloped down, leading way, way deeper than the ocean ridge Aquora was built on. The swordfish dived. The water grew darker.

Far below, Max saw a faint yellow glimmer. As he watched it grew bigger and brighter, until it became a vast undersea city of golden-glinting rock rushing up towards them. There were towers, spires, domes, bridges, courtyards, squares, gardens. A city as big as Aquora, and far more beautiful, at the bottom of the sea.

———

Max gasped in amazement. The water was
dark, but the city emitted a glow of its own
– a warm phosphorescent light that spilled
from the many windows. The rock sparkled.

———

Orange, pink and scarlet corals and seashells decorated the walls in intricate patterns.

"This is – amazing!" he said.

Lia turned round and smiled at him. "It's my home," she said. "Sumara!"

Calling all Adam Blade fans!
We need YOU!

Are you a huge fan of Beast Quest? Is Adam Blade your favourite author? Do you want to know more about his new series, Sea Quest, before anybody else IN THE WORLD?

We're looking for 100 of the most loyal Adam Blade fans to become Sea Quest Cadets.

So how do I become a Sea Quest Cadet?

Simply go to **www.seaquestbooks.co.uk** and fill in the form.

What do I get if I become a Sea Quest Cadet?

You will be one of a limited number of people to receive exclusive Sea Quest merchandise.

What do I have to do as a Sea Quest Cadet?
Take part in Sea Quest activities with your friends!

ENROL TODAY!
SEA QUEST NEEDS YOU!